Bamboozled

adapted by Tish Rabe
from a script by Denise Fordham

illustrated by
Christopher Moroney

A GOLDEN BOOK • NEW YORK

Based in part on *The Cat in the Hat Knows a Lot About That!* TV series (Episode 118) © CITH Productions, Inc. (a subsidiary of Portfolio Entertainment, Inc.), and Red Hat Animation, Ltd. (a subsidiary of Collingwood O'Hare Productions, Ltd.), 2010–2011.

THE CAT IN THE HAT KNOWS A LOT ABOUT THAT! logo and word mark TM 2010 Dr. Seuss Enterprises, L.P., Portfolio Entertainment, Inc., and Collingwood O'Hare Productions, Ltd. All rights reserved. The PBS KIDS logo is a registered trademark of PBS. Both are used with permission. All rights reserved.

Broadcast in Canada by Treehouse™. Treehouse™ is a trademark of the Corus® Entertainment Inc. group of companies. All rights reserved.

Seussville.com   pbskids.org/catinthehat   treehousetv.com

ISBN: 978-0-375-87307-2
Library of Congress Control Number: 2010930715
Printed in the United States of America   10 9 8 7 6 5 4 3 2 1
Random House Children's Books supports the First Amendment and celebrates the right to read.

"Today's Pammy's birthday," said Sally. "She's two. I don't know what she'd like for a present. Do you?"

"For my birthday," said Nick,
"I got a new bike,
but I have no idea
what a panda would like.

Whatever we get her
we need right away.
We have to get Pammy
a present today!"

"Need a present?" the Cat asked.
"I know what to do.
Today we will fly to
Bam-wam-a-boo-boo.

As soon as we get there,
I'll introduce you
to my good friend—a panda—
whose name is Zhu Zhu.

I'm sure that Zhu Zhu
can help with our quest.
She can tell us what present
a panda likes best."

Soon they landed and
started to look for Zhu Zhu.
"These plants," said the Cat,
"are a grass called bamboo.

Bamboo grows fast and
it's tall and it's thick."
"Too high to see over
to find Zhu Zhu!" said Nick.

"This bamboo is growing
right up to the sky."
"Watch this!" said the Cat.
"I know what we can try!"

"Bamboo stilts!" said the Cat.
"Now I see everywhere.
I think Zhu Zhu lives in
the bamboo over there."

The Cat started to wobble.
The stilts started to sway.
"Watch out!" Sally cried.
"The Cat's coming this way!"

That Cat didn't panic.
He knew what to do.
He reached out and grabbed
a strong piece of bamboo.

Bamboo can bend and
the Cat held on tight.
He flew through the air.
Then he flew out of sight!

"Are you all right?" asked Nick.
"Yes, I'm fine," said the Cat.
"When I visit Zhu Zhu,
I always do that.

And look, I found something
I'd like to show you.
It's a back scratcher made
from a piece of bamboo.

Bamboo is hollow and
it's very light.
I can reach every itch
on the left and the right!

Give it a try.
You will love it, I know."
"I don't see it," said Sally.
"Where did it go?"

"You know, Sally," said Nick,
"this really is weird.
That bamboo back scratcher
just disappeared!"

The bamboo started rustling
and shuffling around.
"I think," Sally said, "that
Zhu Zhu has been found."

Sure enough, it was Zhu Zhu!
The kids smiled at her—
a beautiful panda
with black-and-white fur.

"Here's your back scratcher,"
said Zhu Zhu. "It's true.
I love anything
that is made of bamboo."

She did something next
that was quite a surprise
as Sally and Nick looked on
with wide eyes!

She took the back scratcher
and bit it in two!
"Is this something," asked Nick,
"that you usually do?"

"I eat lots of bamboo," she said.
"I peel it and chew it.
With our strong teeth and jaws,
all pandas can do it."

Sally said, "We need a present
for Pammy Panda, our friend.
Is there something special
that you'd recommend?"

"Well," said Zhu Zhu,
"what I would suggest
is a gift of bamboo.
That's what pandas like best."

"Zhu Zhu," cried the Cat,
"meet Thing One and Thing Two!
They are experts on what
can be made from bamboo.

Pandas eat mostly
bamboo, that is true,
but bamboo can be made
into other things, too!

Bamboo drums, picture frames,
bicycles, and a fence.
Bamboo lamps are on sale now
for ninety-nine cents!"

"When I blow through bamboo,"
Sally said, "I can hear
a musical sound that is
pretty and clear."

"When I bang on these big
bamboo drums with a stick,
I can beat out a really
great rhythm!" said Nick.

They began making music!
Though it wasn't planned,
they soon put together
the All-Bamboo Band.

The Cat started to sing.
That Cat couldn't be stopped.
But when it comes to singing,
the Cat can't be topped!

He sang, "Our world's better
because of bamboo.
It bends and it's hollow.
It's light and strong, too.

Pandas eat it all day.
They can peel it and chew it,
and we can make music
by blowing air through it!"

"I loved your bamboo song,"
Zhu Zhu said. "To thank you
here's a present for Pammy—
a bunch of bamboo.

It's tough and it's tall.
It bends and it's sweet.
And for pandas like us,
it's the best food to eat."

Back home, Nick said, "Pammy,
this present's for you,
from a panda who lives
in Bam-wam-a-boo-boo.

She told us that pandas
eat mostly bamboo.
It's just right for her,
so it's just right for you."

"Pammy knows," said the Cat,
"bamboo's what pandas need."
"She said that?" asked Sally.
And the Cat said, "Indeed."